Dessert Time

Dessert Time

Over 200 Fabulous Dessert Recipes

by Rivky Katz

THE JUDAICA PRESS, INC.

Dessert Time

Other cookbooks by Rivky Katz: Salad Time 1, Salad Time 2

ISBN: 978-1-60763-026-5
Proofreader: Hadassa Goldsmith
Cover design and layout: Justine Elliott

THE JUDAICA PRESS, INC.
123 Ditmas Avenue / Brooklyn, NY 11218
718-972-6200 / 800-972-6201
info@judaicapress.com
www.judaicapress.com

Manufactured in the United States of America

Contents

Cakes

Amaretto Cake

2 c. flour
2 c. sugar
2 tsp. baking powder
2/3 c. oil
4 eggs
1 packet vanilla instant pudding
3/4 c. orange juice
1/4 c. vodka
1/4 c. amaretto

Mix all ingredients. Pour into 9" x 13" pan and bake at 350° for 1 hour.

Apple Cake

2 c. flour
2 c. sugar
1 c. oil
4 eggs
2 1/2 tsp. baking powder
1/2 c. orange juice

Filling:
5 apples, sliced
2 T. sugar
dash of cinnamon

Mix cake ingredients. Pour half of cake mixture into 9" x 13" pan. Combine filling ingredients and pour on top. Then pour rest of cake mixture on top of filling. Bake at 350° for 1 hour.

Apple Crisp

1 stick margarine
1 c. sugar
¾ c. flour
½ tsp. cinnamon
4-5 apples, sliced
½ c. orange juice

Mix first four ingredients by hand to make crumbs. Place half of crumb mixture into 9" round pan. Put sliced applies on top and then rest of crumbs. Pour orange juice on top. Bake at 350° for 45 minutes to 1 hour.

Apple Strudel

4-5 cortland apples, grated
1 c. brown sugar
⅓ stick margarine
½ tsp. cinnamon
½ tsp. salt
Juice of 1 lemon
1 pkg. vanilla sugar
2 T. flour
1 pkg. Mazor's flaky dough

Boil first seven ingredients in pot. After ingredients are boiled, add flour. Mix well. Let cool. Fill rolled-out dough. Roll dough into a log and brush top with egg. Bake at 425° for 10 minutes, and then lower to 350° for 30 minutes.

Blondies

1 stick margarine
3/4 c. sugar
3/4 c. brown sugar
2 eggs
1 pkg. vanilla sugar
1 tsp. baking soda
pinch of salt
2½ c. flour
6 oz. chocolate chips

Cream margarine, and then add rest of ingredients. Mix well. Pour into greased 9" x 13" pan and bake at 350° for 40 minutes.

Blueberry Cake

1 stick margarine
1 c. orange juice
2 tsp. baking powder
3 c. flour
1 tsp. vanilla sugar
1 egg
1½ c. sugar
1 c. fresh blueberries, or as desired to taste

Cream margarine, then add rest of ingredients except for blueberries and mix well. Add blueberries by hand. Pour into two 9" round pans or one 9" x 13" pan.

Topping:
1 T. margarine
½ tsp. cinnamon
2 T. flour
2 T. sugar

Combine topping ingredients and sprinkle on top. Bake at 350° for 1½ hours.

Brownie Mousse Trifle

1 box Duncan Hines® brownie mix

Follow box directions and bake in two 9" round pans.

Mousse:

1½ c. marshmallow fluff
2½ bars Rosemarie® chocolate
½ c. coffee whitener
8 oz. whip topping

Mix together first three ingredients. In another bowl, whip up whip topping. In a trifle bowl, place one layer of brownie cake, followed by a layer of mousse and a layer of whip topping. Then repeat: brownie cake, mousse and topping. Refrigerate.

Brownies 1

1½ c. flour
2 c. sugar
⅔ c. oil
1 tsp. baking powder
4 eggs
¾ c. cocoa

Mix all ingredients by hand. Spread into 9" x 13" pan and bake at 350° for 30-45 minutes.

Brownies 2

¾ c. oil
2 c. sugar
1 c. flour
1 c. cocoa
4 egg whites
2 tsp. vanilla extract
pinch of salt

Mix all ingredients. Spread into 8" x 8" pan and bake at 350° for 30 minutes.

Brownies 3

1 c. oil
2 c. sugar
1 tsp. vanilla sugar
4 eggs
2 c. flour
¾ c. cocoa
½ tsp. baking powder

Combine oil and sugar, and then add vanilla sugar and one egg at a time, mixing well. Add rest of ingredients and mix well. Spread into greased 9" x 13" pan and bake at 350° for 35 minutes.

Brownies 4

1 c. margarine
2 c. sugar
2 tsp. vanilla sugar
4 eggs
1 c. flour
⅔ c. cocoa
½ tsp. baking powder

Cream margarine, sugar and vanilla well, and then add eggs. Gradually combine with rest of ingredients. Spread into greased 9" x 13" pan and bake for 25 minutes or until done.

Brownies 5

4 eggs
¾ c. oil
1 tsp. vanilla sugar
2 c. sugar
½ c. cocoa
1½ c. flour
1 T. baking powder

Mix all ingredients by hand. Pour into 9" x 13" pan and bake at 350° for 35-40 minutes.

Brownies 6

4 eggs
2 c. sugar
⅔ c. cocoa
⅔ c. oil
2 tsp. vanilla sugar
1 tsp. baking powder
1 tsp. coffee
¼ c. orange juice
1 c. flour

Mix all ingredients. Pour into 9" x 13" pan and bake at 350° for 30 minutes.

Caramel Chocolate Chip Cake

2 c. flour
1 c. light brown sugar
½ c. white sugar
½ c. finely chopped chocolate chips
½ c. shortening
1¼ c. coffee rich
1 tsp. salt
½ tsp. baking soda
1½ tsp. vanilla sugar
3 eggs
1 tsp. baking powder

Mix all ingredients. Pour into 9" x 13" pan and bake at 350° for 40-45 minutes.

Carrot Muffins 1

4 jars baby food carrots
4 eggs
1 c. oil
2 c. flour
1 tsp. salt
1 c. sugar
1 tsp. baking powder
1 tsp. baking soda
2 T. vanilla sugar

Mix all ingredients. Pour into greased muffin tins and bake at 350° for 50-60 minutes.

Carrot Muffins 2

1 c. sugar
2 jars baby food carrots
½ c. oil
1½ c. flour
1 tsp. baking powder
1 tsp. baking soda
1 tsp. cinnamon
2 eggs

Mix all ingredients. Pour into greased muffin tins and bake at 350° until brown on top.

Chocolate Cake 1

1 c. oil
4 eggs
2½ c. sugar
2 tsp. baking powder
2 tsp. baking soda
1 tsp. vanilla
3 c. flour
2 c. coffee, made
1 c. cocoa

Mix all ingredients. Pour into 9" x 13" pan and bake at 325° for 35 minutes.

Chocolate Cake 2

2¼ c. flour
1¾ c. sugar
⅔ c. cocoa
2 tsp. coffee
1 tsp. baking powder
1 tsp. baking soda
¾ tsp. salt
3 eggs
1½ c. water
1¼ c. oil

Mix all ingredients well, and then slowly add oil. Pour into 9" x 13" pan and bake at 350° for 45 minutes.

Topping:
½ small jar marshmallow fluff
8 oz. whip topping

Mix topping ingredients. When cake has cooled, spread topping over cake.

Chocolate Chip Blondies

¼ c. margarine
1 c. light brown sugar
1 egg
1 c. flour
¼ tsp. baking soda
¼ tsp. salt
¼ c. chocolate chips
½ c. walnuts

Preheat oven to 350°. Cream margarine and brown sugar, and then add egg. Combine flour, baking soda and salt and add to batter. Do not over mix. Fold in chips and walnuts. Spread into greased 8" square pan and bake for 25 minutes.

Chocolate Chip Cake

2 sticks margarine
¾ c. brown sugar
¾ c. sugar
1 tsp. vanilla extract
2 eggs
2¼ c. flour
1 tsp. baking soda
1 tsp. salt
10 oz. chocolate chips

Cream margarine, and then add brown sugar and plain sugar and mix well. Add rest of ingredients, and then mix in chocolate chips by hand. Spread onto greased 9" x 13" pan, and bake at 350° for 30-40 minutes.

Chocolate Chip Muffins

11 T. margarine
2 c. sugar
4 c. flour
4 eggs
1½ c. orange juice
2 tsp. vanilla sugar
6 tsp. baking powder
12 oz. chocolate chips

Cream margarine and sugar well, and then add rest of ingredients except chocolate chips. Fold in chocolate chips. Pour into greased cupcake holders and bake at 350° for 45 minutes.

Chocolate-Covered Pound Cake

6 eggs
2 c. sugar
1 c. oil
2 tsp. vanilla sugar
1½ c. flour
1 tsp. baking powder

Topping:
confection sugar
6 oz. chocolate, melted

Mix all ingredients and pour into greased bundt pan. Bake at 350° for 1 hour. When cooled, sprinkle confection sugar on top and drizzle chocolate over sugar.

Chocolate Devil Cake

1 c. margarine
1 c. cocoa
2 c. hot water
2½ c. sugar
1 ½ tsp. baking powder
1 tsp. baking soda
2½ c. flour
½ tsp. salt
5 eggs
2 tsp. vanilla extract

Cream margarine first, and then add rest of ingredients, adding one egg at a time and mixing well. Pour into 9" x 13" pan or bundt pan and bake at 350° for 55 minutes or until done.

Chocolate Mousse Brownies

½ c. margarine
12 oz. chocolate chips
2 c. sugar
1½ c. flour
2 tsp. vanilla sugar
½ tsp. baking powder
½ tsp. salt
3 eggs
½ c. chopped pecans

Melt together margarine and chocolate chips. Combine with rest of ingredients except pecans. When batter is smooth, fold in pecans. Spread into greased 9" x 13" pan.

Mouse Topping:
¾ c. whip topping
6 oz. chocolate chips
3 eggs
1½ tsp. vanilla sugar
½ c. sugar
¼ tsp. salt
1 c. chopped pecans

Melt chocolate chips with whip topping. Allow to cool slightly. Mix all other ingredients except pecans in bowl and beat until foamy, then stir in chocolate mixture. Pour mousse topping over brownie batter, and then sprinkle with pecans. Bake at 350° for 1 hour. Allow to cool before cutting.

Chocolate Mousse Cake

4 oz. margarine
7 oz. chocolate (from high quality bars)
7 eggs, separated
¾ c. sugar
1 tsp. vanilla extract
3 T. wine

Melt together margarine and chocolate over low flame for 5 minutes, or until melted. Beat egg whites with ¼ c. sugar until stiff. In another bowl, beat egg yolks with ½ c. sugar until thick. Add vanilla extract and wine to chocolate mixture and combine with egg yolk mixture. Fold into egg white mixture. Pour half of batter into 9" round pan and bake at 350° for 35 minutes. When cake is cool, pour rest of batter on top and freeze.

Corn Muffins

1 c. flour
¾ c. corn meal
4 T. sugar
1 T. baking powder
1 tsp. salt
1 egg
⅔ c. coffee whitener
⅓ c. oil

Preheat oven to 425°. Grease muffin pans. Mix flour, corn meal, sugar, baking power and salt by hand. In another bowl, mix egg, coffee whitener and oil. Combine both mixtures well. Pour into greased muffin tins ⅔ full and bake for 20 minutes.

Cream Puffs

1 c. water
½ c. margarine
1 c. flour
½ tsp. salt
4 eggs

Preheat oven to 400°. Combine water and margarine and melt over low heat. Stir in flour and salt until smooth ball forms. Remove from heat. Mix in egg one at a time. Spoon onto cookie sheet and bake for 30 minutes. Prick top of puffs to let out steam. When cool, cut puffs in half and fill with desired cream or ice cream. Drizzle with chocolate syrup.

Crumb Cake 1

1½ sticks margarine
4 c. flour
2 c. sugar
2 T. vanilla sugar
½ c. oil
1 c. orange juice
4 tsp. baking powder

Cream margarine, then mix in flour, sugar, vanilla sugar and oil. Separate and set aside 1 cup of this mixture for crumbs. Add eggs, orange juice and baking powder to remaining mixture. Pour into greased pan and sprinkle crumbs on top. Bake at 350° for 45 minutes or until brown.

Crumb Cake 2

½ c. oil
1 stick margarine
1 T. vanilla sugar
2 tsp. baking powder
½ tsp. salt
3 c. flour
1½ c. sugar
3 eggs
8 oz. whip topping

Mix first seven ingredients to form a crumb mixture. Remove 1 cup of crumb mixture and set aside. To remaining mixture, add eggs and whip topping. Mix well and then pour into 9" x 13" pan. Sprinkle crumb mixture on top. Bake at 350° for 40 minutes.

Cupcakes

2 c. sugar
3 eggs
1½ c. coffee whitener
⅔ c. Crisco®
½ tsp. vanilla sugar
2¾ c. flour

Mix all ingredients and pour into cupcake holders. Bake at 350° for 25 minutes.

Frosted Chocolate Cake

2 c. sugar
1¾ c. flour
¾ c. cocoa
1 ½ tsp. baking powder
1 ½ tsp. baking soda
2 eggs
1 c. coffee whitener
½ c. oil
2 tsp. vanilla sugar
1 c. boiling water
1 tsp. salt

Mix all ingredients. Pour into 9" x 13" greased pan and bake at 350° for 1 hour.

Frosting:
1 stick margarine
⅔ c. cocoa
3 c. confection sugar
⅓ c. coffee whitener
1 tsp. vanilla extract

Cream margarine and then add rest of ingredients. If too stiff, add more coffee whitener. Frost cake after it has cooled.

Honey Cake

½ c. oil
1½ c. brown sugar
1 tsp. cinnamon
3 eggs
1 c. honey
2½ tsp. coffee in 1 c. boiled water
1½ tsp. baking soda
3 c. flour

Mix all ingredients and bake at 350° for 45 minutes to 1 hour.

Kokosh Cake

Dough:

5 lbs. flour
2 lbs. margarine
1¾ c. sugar
3½ c. water
4 oz. yeast
1 tsp. vanilla sugar
5 eggs
1 c. orange juice
1 ½ tsp. salt

Filling:

2 c. cocoa
6 c. sugar
½ c. flour
2 T. vanilla sugar

Topping:

⅓ c. margarine
½ c. sugar
¾ c. flour
½ T. cinnamon

Mix dough well. Divide dough into four equal portions. Roll each part into a rectangle. Mix together filling ingredients, and then sprinkle each dough with filling and roll "jelly roll" style, starting from the wide end. Bake as is to make four rolls, or braid the rolls into two large loaves. Mix together topping ingredients and sprinkle on top. Bake at 350° for 1 hour.

Mandel Bread

3 eggs
2 tsp. vanilla sugar
3/4 c. oil
3/4 c. sugar
3/4 c. flour
2 tsp. baking powder
dash of salt

Topping:
Sugar, to taste
Cinnamon, to taste (should be equal to the amount of sugar)

Mix all cake ingredients and form into six loaves. Place on ungreased baking sheet and sprinkle mixture of sugar and cinnamon on top. Bake at 350° for 20 minutes and remove from oven. Slice loaves and lay pieces flat on pan. Put back in oven for 10 more minutes.

Marble Almond Cake

7 eggs
2 c. flour
2 c. sugar
2 tsp. baking powder
1 c. oil
1 vanilla sugar

Mix all ingredients and pour 2/3 of batter into 9" x 13" pan. To remaining batter, add:

1/2 c. cocoa
1/4 c. water
2 T. almond extract
2 T. sugar

Swirl into pan to marbleize and bake at 350° for 45 minutes.

Marble Bundt Cake 1

1 c. oil
6 eggs
2 c. sugar
2 c. flour
1 tsp. baking powder
2 tsp. vanilla sugar
2 T. cocoa

Mix all ingredients except cocoa and pour ⅔ of batter into greased bundt pan. Add cocoa to remaining batter and swirl into pan to marbleize. Bake at 350° for 50 minutes.

Marble Bundt Cake 2

8 eggs, separated
2 c. sugar
½ c. orange juice
¾ c. oil
2 c. flour
1 tsp. baking powder
1 vanilla sugar
3 T. cocoa

Whip egg whites until stiff and gradually add 1 c. sugar. Beat yolks with rest of sugar, orange juice, oil, flour, baking powder and vanilla sugar. Fold batter into egg whites mixture. Coat bundt pan with flour and margarine and pour half of batter into pan. Add cocoa to remaining batter and swirl into pan to marbleize. Bake at 350° for 1 hour.

Marble Cake

2 c. sugar
1 c. oil
6 eggs
1 tsp. baking powder
1½ c. flour
2 tsp. vanilla extract
3-4 T. cocoa

Mix all ingredients except cocoa. Pour ⅔ of batter into 9" x 13" greased pan. Add cocoa to remaining batter and swirl into pan to marbleize. Bake at 350° for 45 minutes to 1 hour.

Marshmallow Cake

½ c. margarine
¾ c. sugar
2 eggs
¾ tsp. baking powder
1 tsp. vanilla sugar
¾ c. flour
2 tsp. cocoa
1 small jar marshmallow fluff

Cream margarine and add in all ingredients except marshmallow fluff. Pour into 9" x 13" pan and bake at 350° for 20 minutes. Remove from oven and spread on fluff while cake is hot. Freeze for 1 hour.

Topping:
6 oz. chocolate chips
1 c. peanut butter
¾ c. Rice Krispies®

Melt together chocolate and peanut butter and add Rice Krispies. Spread on top of cake and refreeze.

Marshmallow Miniatures

Bake chocolate cake (any recipe) on cookie sheet. While cake is hot, spread half of large jar of marshmallow fluff on top and freeze for 3 hours or overnight.

Melt:
12 oz. white chocolate
12 oz. peanut butter
3 c. Rice Krispies®

Using wax paper, press mixture onto the cake and then refreeze. Before serving, drizzle with chocolate and cut into circles.

No-Rise Rugelach

½ c. lukewarm water
1½ T. dry yeast
3 sticks margarine
¼ c. sugar
1 egg
4 c. flour
pinch of salt
2 tsp. vanilla sugar

Filling:
⅔ c. sugar
⅔ c. brown sugar
¼ c. ground walnuts
2 tsp. cinnamon

Dissolve yeast in water. Cream margarine together with sugar and egg. Mix in rest of ingredients. Divide into 4 parts. Roll out each part and brush with oil. Sprinkle each part with filling. Roll up each part "jelly roll" style beginning with the wider end. Bake at 350° until brown on top.

Orange Pound Cake

6 eggs
2 c. sugar
2 tsp. vanilla extract or pound cake extract
1 c. oil
3 c. flour
pinch of salt
3 tsp. baking powder
1 c. orange juice
confection sugar

Combine eggs, sugar, extract and oil. Gradually mix in flour, salt and baking powder, and then beat in orange juice until smooth. Pour batter into greased bundt pan and bake at 350° for 1 hour and 10 minutes. Sprinkle with confection sugar.

Pareve Cheesecake 1

16 oz. pareve cream cheese
16 oz. whip topping
3 eggs
1 vanilla sugar
⅔ c. sugar
1 T. lemon juice
2 graham cracker piecrusts

Mix all ingredients and divide into two crusts. Bake at 350° for 1 hour.

Pareve Cheesecake 2

16 oz. pareve cream cheese
3 eggs
1 tsp. vanilla sugar
1 T. lemon juice
¾ c. sugar
1 unbaked piecrust

Mix all ingredients and pour into piecrust. Preheat oven to 375° for 15 minutes, and then lower to 350°. Bake pie for 30 minutes.

Pareve Cheesecake 3

8 oz. pareve cream cheese
2 eggs
1 tsp. vanilla sugar
1 tsp. lemon juice
½ c. sugar
1 unbaked piecrust

Mix all ingredients and pour into piecrust. Bake at 350° for 45 minutes.

Pecan Brownies

½ c. margarine
12 oz. chocolate chips
2 c. sugar
1½ c. flour
2 tsp. vanilla sugar
½ tsp. baking powder
½ tsp. salt
3 eggs
½ c. chopped pecans

Melt together margarine and chocolate chips. Stir in rest of ingredients except pecans. When mixed well, stir in pecans. Pour into 9" x 13" pan and bake at 350° for 50 minutes.

Pound Cake 1

6 eggs
1¼ c. sugar
½ c. oil
1 tsp. almond extract
2 tsp. vanilla sugar
1 tsp. salt
2 c. flour
3 tsp. baking powder
¾ c. cold water

Beat eggs with sugar and then add remaining ingredients. Pour into greased tube pan and bake at 350° for 1 hour.

Pound Cake 2

6 eggs
1¼ c. sugar
½ c. oil
1 tsp. almond extract
2 c. flour
3 tsp. baking powder
1 tsp. salt
2 tsp. vanilla sugar
¾ c. orange juice

Beat eggs with sugar and then add oil and almond extract. Combine baking powder, salt, vanilla sugar and flour, adding in the orange juice alternately with flour. Pour into 9" x 13" pan or tube pan and bake at 350° for 1 hour.

Strawberry Shortcake

9 eggs, separated
1 c. sugar
1 c. flour
⅓ c. orange juice
1 vanilla sugar
1 tsp. baking powder

Topping:
16 oz. whip topping
4 T. confection sugar
1 box fresh strawberries

Whip egg whites and ½ c. sugar until stiff. Add rest of ingredients. Add flour and sugar slowly, mixing well. Pour into greased tube pan and bake at 350° for 1 hour. Remove from oven and turn cake upside-down for 2 hours. When cool, slice cake in half. Top one half of cake with whip topping and sliced strawberries, and then place other half of cake on top. Dust with confection sugar. Alternatively, use some whip topping to cream outside of cake, and place 2 or 3 sliced strawberries on top for garnish.

Vanilla Cake

1½ c. flour
6 eggs
2 c. sugar
1 c. oil
1 tsp. baking powder
2 tsp. vanilla sugar

Topping:
confection sugar
chocolate, melted

Mix all cake ingredients. Pour into greased bundt pan and bake at 350° for 1 hour. When cool, sprinkle cake with confection sugar and drizzle melted chocolate on top.

Vanilla Cream Cake

Cake:

6 eggs
1½ c. sugar
¼ c. oil
2 tsp. vanilla sugar
1½ c. flour
2 tsp. baking powder

Beat eggs and sugar, and then add rest of ingredients. Bake on greased cookie sheet (12" x 16" pan) at 350° for 15-20 minutes.

Filling:

20 oz. whip topping
½ c. cold water
1 pkg. instant vanilla pudding
½ tsp. vanilla extract

Beat all ingredients together.

Topping:

1 stick margarine
6 T. cocoa
3 T. coffee whitener
3 T. water
1 tsp. vanilla extract
confection sugar

Combine first four ingredients in a pot and bring to a boil. Remove from heat, add vanilla extract and slowly add confection sugar until slightly thickened. When cake has cooled, spread filling on top and freeze. When frozen, spread topping on top, cover and refreeze.

Warm Chocolate Fudge Cake

2 c. flour
4 tsp. baking powder
1 tsp. salt
1⅓ c. sugar
4 T. cocoa
1 c. coffee whitener
2 tsp. vanilla sugar
4 T. oil
2 c. brown sugar
½ c. cocoa
3 c. boiling water

Combine flour, baking powder, salt, sugar and cocoa in bowl. In another bowl, mix coffee whitener, vanilla sugar and oil. Combine dry ingredients with wet ingredients and mix well. Place in 9" x 13" ungreased pan. Sprinkle brown sugar and cocoa over cake batter. Pour boiling water on top until bubbles form. Bake at 350° for 45 minutes. Serve warm.

Yellow Cupcakes

2 c. sugar
3 eggs
1½ c. coffee whitener
⅔ c. Crisco®
½ tsp. vanilla sugar
2¾ c. flour

Mix all ingredients and pour into cupcake holders ¾ full. Bake at 350° for 25 minutes. Frost if desired.

Zucchini Muffins

3 eggs
¾ c. oil
1¾ c. sugar
2 c. zucchini, grated
2 tsp. vanilla sugar
2 tsp. baking soda
1½ tsp. cinnamon
¼ tsp. baking powder
½ tsp. salt
2 c. flour

Mix all ingredients in bowl, adding flour last. Pour into greased muffin tins and bake at 350° until muffins turn brown on top.

Chocolate Glaze

1 c. confection sugar
4 T. oil
4 T. cocoa
4 T. hot water

Mix well and pour over cake.

Chocolate Fudge Sauce

½ c. cocoa
¾ c. sugar
½ c. whip topping
½ stick margarine
1 scoop vanilla sugar

Combine all ingredients in pot and simmer over low flame until everything has melted. Pour over cake.

Lemon Frosting

6 T. margarine, softened
1 c. confection sugar
1 lemon rind, grated
1 T. lemon juice

Beat margarine until fluffy. Gradually beat in sugar. Then beat in lemon rind and gradually add lemon juice. Beat well. Frost cake.

Cookies

Apricot Nut Bars

½ lb. margarine
1 c. sugar
2 egg yolks
2 c. flour
1 c. chopped walnuts
½ c. apricot preserves

Cream margarine. Gradually add sugar, and then egg yolks. Blend mixture well. Gradually add flour. Fold in most of the nuts (save some for topping). Spread half of batter [illegible] 8" x 8" pan. Spread apricot preserves on top and then [illegible] of batter. Top with remaining nuts. Bake at 350° for ½ hour or until lightly brown on top. Remove from oven and divide into bars.

Biscotti

½ c. oil
1 c. sugar
2 eggs
1 tsp. vanilla extract
2 c. flour
1 tsp. baking powder
¼ tsp. salt
1 c. chocolate chips

Topping:
4 T. sugar
1 tsp. cinnamon

Preheat oven to 350°. Mix together oil and sugar and then add eggs. Combine with rest of ingredients, adding chocolate chips last. Shape dough into 4 loaves and place on cookie sheet lined with parchment paper. Mix sugar and cinnamon and sprinkle on loaves. Bake 30-40 minutes. Slice while warm and place in cold oven for a few hours.

Cherry Squares

1½ c. sugar
2 sticks margarine
4 eggs
2 c. flour
2 T. lemon juice
cherry pie filling

Cream sugar and margarine. Add eggs, flour and lemon juice, and mix well. Pour batter onto greased cookie sheet, and make lines to form squares. Put one cherry (from the pie filling) in each square. Bake at 350° for 25 minutes. Cool and cut into squares.

Chocolate Chip Cookies 1

2 sticks margarine
1½ c. brown sugar
½ tsp. salt
1 tsp. baking soda
2½ tsp. vanilla sugar
2 tsp. baking powder
2⅓ c. flour
12 oz. white chocolate chips
2 c. Rice Krispies®
2 eggs

Cream margarine, and then add rest of ingredients and mix together. Scoop balls onto greased cookie sheet, keeping them spread apart. Bake at 350° for 10-15 minutes.

Chocolate Chip Cookies 2

1 c. shortening
1 c. brown sugar
½ c. sugar
2 eggs
1 tsp. salt
1 tsp. baking soda
1 tsp. vanilla sugar
2 c. flour
10 oz. chocolate chips

Mix all ingredients. Roll into balls and pat down slightly. Place onto lined cookie sheet and bake at 350° for 8-10 minutes.

Chocolate Chip Cookies 3

1 stick shortening
¾ c. sugar
¾ c. brown sugar
1 tsp. vanilla sugar
2 eggs
1 tsp. baking soda
2½ c. flour
pinch of salt
2 c. chocolate chips

Beat shortening with sugar and brown sugar. Add vanilla sugar and eggs. Combine with rest of dry ingredients, adding chocolate chips last. Shape into balls and place on cookie sheet lined with baking paper and sprayed with oil. Bake at 350° for 12-15 minutes.

Chocolate Chip Cookies 4

2¼ c. flour
⅓ c. cocoa
1 tsp. baking soda
½ tsp. salt
2 sticks margarine
¾ c. sugar
¾ c. light brown sugar
1 tsp. vanilla sugar
2 eggs
24 oz. chocolate chips

Mix flour, cocoa, baking soda and salt. In another bowl, beat margarine, sugar, brown sugar and vanilla sugar on medium speed until creamy. Add eggs and gradually stir in dry ingredients. Mix in chocolate chips. Drop onto ungreased cookie sheet and bake at 375° for 8-10 minutes.

Chocolate Clusters

12 oz. chocolate chips
½ c. peanut butter
½ c. almonds
1 c. Rice Krispies®

Melt together chocolate and peanut butter. Mix in rest of ingredients. Drop spoonfuls onto ungreased cookie sheet and freeze.

Chocolate Crunchies

4 oz. margarine
4 oz. sugar
4 T. corn syrup
4 T. cocoa
5 C. corn flakes

Melt first four ingredients in pot over low heat. Remove pot from heat and add in corn flakes. Mix well. Roll into balls, place in cupcake holders and refrigerate.

Chocolate Fudge

1/3 c. cocoa
2/3 c. sugar
1/3 c. dessert whip
2 T. margarine
1 tsp. vanilla extract

Boil first 4 ingredients, stirring until sugar has melted, and then add vanilla extract. Refrigerate.

Chocolate Peanut Butter Crunch

6 oz. baking chocolate, chopped
2 sticks unsalted margarine
16 oz. jar creamy peanut butter
3 c. Rice Krispies®
1/4 tsp. salt
3 c. confection sugar

Line 8" square pan with parchment paper. Melt chocolate and 1 tablespoon margarine over low heat. Remove from heat and stir in half of peanut butter and 2 cups Rice Krispies. Spread mixture evenly in pan. Refrigerate for 15 minutes to harden. In pot, combine remainder of margarine and salt, and heat until melted. Remove from heat. Add rest of peanut butter and confection sugar and mix until smooth. Spread over Rice Krispies mixture and refrigerate another 15 minutes or until hard. Cut into squares.

Chocolate Peanut Chews

1 c. light corn syrup
1 c. sugar
1 c. peanut butter
5 c. Rice Krispies®

In pot, bring corn syrup and sugar to a boil. Remove from heat, mix in peanut butter and Rice Krispies and spread onto cookie sheet.

Topping:
8 oz. bittersweet chocolate
1 oz. margarine

Melt chocolate with margarine and spread mixture on top.

Chocolate Treats

1 c. water
2 T. cocoa
2 tsp. vanilla extract
2 sticks margarine
4 eggs
1 c. sugar

Blend all ingredients in blender. Pour into 9" x 13" pan and freeze. Cut into small squares when frozen and place into mini cupcake holders.

Cinnamon Cookies

3 eggs
1 c. sugar
3/4 c. oil
2 tsp. baking powder
3 c. flour
1/2 c. sugar
2 tsp. cinnamon

Mix eggs, sugar and oil, and then add baking powder and flour. Shape into walnut-size balls. Roll in mixture of cinnamon and sugar and flatten with fork. Place onto lined cookie sheet and bake at 375° for 10-12 minutes.

Coconut Macaroons

3 c. coconut flakes
1½ T. cornstarch
¾ c. sugar
½ tsp. vanilla
3 egg whites
1 bar Noblesse® bittersweet chocolate

Mix coconut, cornstarch, sugar, vanilla and egg whites in bowl. Set bowl over a pot of boiling water until mixture thickens. Drop tablespoonfuls onto ungreased baking sheet and bake at 350° for 10-15 minutes. Remove from oven and place macaroons onto wire rack to cool. Melt chocolate and dip in only bottoms of macaroons. Place on waxed paper and refrigerate to set.

Colored Chocolate Chip Cookies

1 stick margarine
1 c. sugar
1 egg
1 tsp. vanilla extract
1 c. flour
½ c. cocoa
½ tsp. baking soda
less than ½ tsp. salt
1 c. colored chocolate chips or white chocolate chips

Beat margarine and sugar until creamy, and then add egg and vanilla extract. Mix in remaining ingredients. Roll into small balls and place on ungreased cookie sheet. Bake for 10-12 minutes and then cool on wire rack.

Crispy Chocolate Chip Cookies

1 c. sugar
1 c. brown sugar
2 sticks margarine
1 egg
1 c. oil
2 tsp. vanilla sugar
3½ c. flour
1 c. rolled oats
1 tsp. baking soda
1 tsp. cream of tartar
8 oz. chocolate chips
1 c. Rice Krispies®

Mix the first six ingredients well. In another bowl, combine together remaining ingredients, then add mixture to first bowl and mix well. Shape into round balls, and then flatten with fork on ungreased, lined cookie sheet. Bake at 350° for 12-15 minutes.

Crunchy Balls

2 c. confection sugar
1 c. honey graham crackers, crushed
¾ c. ground walnuts
½ c. coconut, shredded
½ c. peanut butter
1 stick margarine, melted
1 bar chocolate

Mix all ingredients well. Form into balls and place on baking sheet. Freeze for 1½ hours. Remove from freezer. Melt chocolate over low heat and dip balls into chocolate. Refreeze. Remove from freezer an hour before serving.

Crystal Cookies

1 c. margarine
3/4 c. cornstarch
1/3 c. confection sugar
1 c. flour
3 T. confection sugar
crystal sugars (any 2 colors)

Beat margarine until fluffy, and then add cornstarch and 1/3 cup confection sugar. Add flour, mixing well until it forms a dough. Refrigerate for 1 hour or until chilled. Roll into balls and place on cookie sheet. Combine 3 tablespoons confection sugar with colored crystals and roll cookies in mixture. Bake at 350° until golden brown.

Devil Dogs

1/2 c. Crisco®
1 egg
3/4 tsp. baking soda
1/2 c. cocoa
1 c. sugar
2 c. flour
1 c. water
1/4 tsp. salt

Mix all ingredients. Shape into logs of desired thickness and drop onto greased cookie sheet. Bake at 350° for 15-20 minutes. When cool, slice logs in half lengthwise.

Filling:
1/2 c. Crisco®
1 tsp. vanilla extract
1 small jar marshmallow fluff
1/2 c. confection sugar

Mix all filling ingredients, fill one side of log and cover with other side.

Double Peanut Butter Bars

¾ c. margarine
¾ c. creamy peanut butter
¾ c. sugar
¾ c. brown sugar
2 tsp. water
2 eggs
1½ tsp. vanilla sugar
1½ c. flour
1½ c. cooking oats
¾ tsp. baking soda
½ tsp. sale

In bowl, cream margarine, peanut butter, sugar, brown sugar and water. Beat in eggs and vanilla sugar, and then add rest of ingredients. Spread onto cookie sheet and bake at 325° for 18-20 minutes.

Topping:
1¼ c. chocolate chips
½ c. peanut butter

Melt together chocolate chips and peanut butter and spread over warm bars.

Everything Cookies

1 c. margarine, softened
3/4 c. sugar
3/4 c. light brown sugar
1 tsp. vanilla extract
2 eggs
2 1/4 c. flour
1 tsp. baking soda
1/2 tsp. salt
1 c. coconut flakes
1/2 c. chocolate chips
1/2 c. white chocolate chips
1/2 c. oatmeal
1/2 c. raisins
3/4 c. colored sprinkles

Cream margarine, sugar, brown sugar and vanilla extract until fluffy, and then add eggs. In another bowl, combine flour, baking soda and salt. Add flour mixture to creamed mixture and beat well. Stir in remaining ingredients. Drop tablespoonfuls onto lined cookie sheet and bake at 350° for 15-20 minutes or until golden brown on top.

Giant Zebra Fudge Cookies

½ c. oil
2 c. sugar
1 c. cocoa
4 large eggs
2 tsp. vanilla extract
2 c. flour
2 tsp. baking powder
½ tsp. salt
confection sugar

Mix first three ingredients together, and then add eggs and vanilla extract and mix. Add flour, baking powder and salt, and then mix. Put in refrigerator to harden for 1 hour. Preheat oven to 350°. Remove dough from refrigerator and form into balls. Roll in confection sugar and place on cookie sheet, leaving space between each ball. Bake for 10-20 minutes.

Hamentaschen 1

5½ c. flour
2 tsp. baking powder
1 ½ c. sugar
2 tsp. vanilla
½ tsp. salt
1 c. oil
4 eggs
Filling of your choice (jelly, chocolate chips, etc.)

Mix all ingredients until a soft dough forms. Roll out dough. Cut into round circles using a round cookie cutter or glass cup. Add filling and pinch three corners together into a triangular shape. Place on lined cookie sheet and bake at 350° until light brown.

Hamentaschen 2

3 c. flour
2 tsp. baking powder
½ c. sugar
1 stick margarine
3 eggs
1 tsp. vanilla sugar
Filling of your choice (jelly, chocolate chips, etc.)

Mix flour, baking powder and sugar and then add in margarine until crumbly. Add eggs and vanilla sugar and mix well. Roll out dough. Cut into round circles using a round cookie cutter or glass cup. Add filling and pinch three corners together into a triangular shape. Place on lined cookie sheet and bake at 350° until light brown.

Jelly Cookies

2 sticks margarine
½ c. sugar
2½ c. flour
1 egg
1 tsp. vanilla sugar
Filling of your choice (jelly, chocolate chips, etc.)

Cream margarine and sugar. Add flour, egg and vanilla sugar and mix well. Shape into balls and flatten with hand. Make an indentation in middle of each cookie with finger and fill with chocolate or with jelly flavor of your choice. Place onto lined cookie sheet and bake at 350° for 15-20 minutes.

Log Cookies

2 c. flour
2 sticks margarine
½ c. confection sugar
1 tsp. vanilla sugar

Mix all ingredients to form a dough and refrigerate for one hour. Form into 2" logs and place onto lined cookie sheet. Bake at 350° for 12-15 minutes.

Topping:
3½ oz. chocolate bar, melted
Nuts or sprinkles

When cooled, dip ends of cookies into chocolate and then into sprinkles or nuts.

Marble Cookies

1½ sticks margarine
1½ c. sugar
3 c. flour
1¼ tsp. baking soda
1 egg
2 T. water
3 T. cocoa
1 T. oil

Cream margarine and sugar and then mix in flour, baking soda, egg and water. In another bowl, combine cocoa and oil to form a paste. Swirl paste into batter to marbleize. Divide dough into three logs and wrap in saran wrap. Freeze for 2 hours. Cut into 1" slices, place onto cookie sheet and bake at 350° for 12-15 minutes.

Nut Balls

2 sticks margarine, creamed
2 c. flour
1 vanilla sugar
2 c. chopped almonds
3 T. confection sugar

Mix all ingredients except confection sugar and shape into balls. Place onto ungreased cookie sheet and bake at 350° for 25 minutes. Roll in confection sugar while hot.

Nut Cookies

2 sticks margarine
½ c. confection sugar
1 tsp. vanilla extract
2¼ c. flour
¾ c. ground nuts

Cream margarine and then add remainder of ingredients. Drop tablespoonfuls onto cookie sheet and bake at 400° for 10–12 minutes.

Oatmeal Chocolate Chip Cookies 1

¾ c. flour
¾ c. brown sugar
¾ teaspoon baking soda
¾ teaspoon salt
⅓ c. Crisco®
1 egg
1¾ c. quick-cooking oats
¾ c. chocolate chips

Preheat oven to 350°. Mix all ingredients except oats and chocolate chips. When combined well, add oats and chocolate chips by hand. Drop tablespoonfuls onto ungreased cookie sheet and bake for 15 minutes.

Oatmeal Chocolate Chip Cookies 2

1½ c. sugar
2 c. brown sugar
2 c. shortening
1 T. vanilla sugar
4 eggs
6 c. flour
1½ tsp. baking soda
1½ tsp. baking powder
1½ tsp. salt
2½ c. quick-cooking oats
2 c. chocolate chips

Preheat oven to 350°. Cream together plain sugar, brown sugar, shortening and vanilla sugar. Add eggs and mix well. Add flour, baking soda, baking powder, salt and mix well. Add oats and mix well. Add chocolate chips. Scoop golf-ball-size balls onto greased cookie sheet and bake for about 15 minutes or until golden brown.

Oatmeal Raisin Cookies

2 sticks margarine
½ c. sugar
1 c. brown sugar
2 eggs
1 tsp. vanilla sugar
1½ c. flour
1 tsp. baking soda
1 tsp. cinnamon
3 c. oats, uncooked
1 c. raisins

Beat margarine, sugar and brown sugar until creamy. Add eggs and vanilla sugar and beat well. Then add flour, baking soda and cinnamon and mix well. Stir in oats and raisins and mix well. Drop tablespoonfuls onto ungreased cookie sheet and bake for 10-12 minutes until golden brown.

Peanut Butter Balls 1

2 c. crunchy peanut butter
2 c. confection sugar
½ c. margarine, melted
3 c. Rice Krispies®
1 bar bittersweet chocolate

Mix all ingredients and shape into balls. Freeze until hard and then dip in chocolate and refreeze.

Optional: Drizzle white chocolate over balls.

Peanut Butter Balls 2

1½ c. creamy peanut butter
1 stick margarine
1 tsp. vanilla sugar
8 oz. confection sugar

Combine all ingredients in mixer and then roll into small balls. Place into greased 9" x 13" pan and freeze.

Topping:
12 oz. chocolate chips
2 T. shortening

Melt together chocolate chips and shortening. Remove balls from freezer and dip into melted chocolate. Refrigerate until ready to eat.

Peanut Butter Bars

1½ c. peanut butter
16 oz. confection sugar
1 tsp. vanilla sugar
1 stick margarine
12 oz. bag chocolate chips

Mix all ingredients except chocolate chips and press into 9" x 13" pan. Melt chocolate chips and spread over bars. Cut into bars.

Peanut Butter Swirl Bars

2 c. confection sugar
1 c. margarine
½ c. peanut butter

Topping:
6 oz. chocolate chips
6 oz. white chocolate chips

Mix sugar, margarine and peanut butter and spread into a 9" x 13" pan. Refrigerate for 30 minutes. Melt chocolate chips and white chocolate chips in separate pots and drizzle each on top.

Peanut Butter Cookies 1

½ c. margarine
½ c. light brown sugar
½ c. peanut butter
½ tsp. vanilla extract
1 egg
½ tsp. baking soda
½ tsp. salt
1½ c. flour

Cream margarine with sugar and peanut butter and then add vanilla extract and egg. Stir in baking soda and salt and then add flour until a stiff dough forms. Shape into walnut-sized balls, place on lightly greased cookie sheet and press to flatten. Bake at 375° for 10-12 minutes.

Peanut Butter Cookies 2

½ c. peanut butter
¼ c. shortening
¾ c. brown sugar
1 egg
3 T. milk or coffee whitener
1 T. honey
1 T. vanilla sugar
1⅔ c. flour
1 tsp. baking soda
¼ tsp. salt

Mix peanut butter and shortening until creamed and then add brown sugar. Beat in egg and then add rest of ingredients. Shape into little balls and flatten. Place on cookie sheet and bake at 350° for 10-15 minutes.

Peanut Chews

1 c. corn syrup
1 c. peanut butter
1 c. sugar
1 box Rice Krispies®

Mix corn syrup, peanut butter and sugar in pot and bring to a boil. Remove from flame and add Rice Krispies. Spread into 9" x 13" pan and cool.

Pizza Cookie

6 T. margarine
½ c. light brown sugar
¼ c. sugar
1 egg
1 tsp. vanilla extract
1½ c. flour
½ tsp. baking soda
¼ tsp. salt
10 oz. chocolate chips

Preheat oven to 350°. Combine ingredients into a dough. Line round pizza pan with parchment paper. Press down dough firmly into pan, making sure thickness of dough is consistent. Bake 15-20 minutes until lightly browned.

Plain Cookies

4 c. flour
½ box confection sugar
4 eggs
3 T. vanilla extract
2 sticks margarine
1½ tsp. baking powder

Mix all ingredients well. Roll dough into walnut-size balls, place on cookie sheet and flatten slightly with the back of a fork. If desired, sprinkle chocolate chips or sprinkles on top. Bake at 400° degrees until golden brown.

Smore's Bites

3½ oz. bar milk chocolate or dark chocolate
1 bag mini marshmallows
¼ c. chopped walnuts

Line cookie sheet with parchment paper. Melt chocolate and stir in marshmallows and walnuts. Place heaping teaspoons of mixture onto cookie sheet and let chill in refrigerator until set.

Snowballs

2 c. white chocolate chips
2 T. margarine
1 c. shredded coconut
1 c. sponge cake, crumbled
2 T. confection sugar

Melt chocolate chips and margarine. Add ¾ cup coconut and cake crumbs and mix well. Shape mixture into balls and roll balls in remainder of coconut, and then in confection sugar. Place balls onto cookie sheet and refrigerate.

Sugar Cookies 1

2 sticks margarine, softened
2 c. confection sugar
3 eggs
½ tsp. vanilla extract
4 c. flour
1 T. baking powder

Preheat oven to 350°. Cream margarine and confection sugar and then add eggs and vanilla extract. Mix in flour and baking powder to form a dough. Roll out dough and cut into desired shapes using cookie cutters. Place cookies on cookie sheet and bake for 10 minutes. Remove from oven and let cool.

Sugar Cookies 2

1 c. sugar
3 c. flour
2 sticks margarine
2 eggs
2 T. vanilla sugar
2 tsp. baking powder
pinch of salt

Mix all ingredients until a smooth dough is formed. Roll out and cut into desired shapes using cookie cutters. Place cookies onto cookie sheet sprayed with Pam. Sprinkle with sugar and bake at 350° for 20-25 minutes or until golden brown.

Sugar Cookies 3

2 sticks margarine
1 c. sugar
1 egg
1 tsp. baking powder
1 T. orange juice
1 tsp. vanilla sugar
2½ c. flour

Cream together margarine, sugar and egg. Then add rest of ingredients and mix well. Drop tablespoonfuls (or roll into walnut-size balls and flatten slightly with the back of a fork) onto cookie sheet and bake at 400° for 6-10 minutes.

Toffee Bars

1¾ c. flour
1 c. sugar
2 sticks margarine
1 tsp. vanilla extract
1 large egg, separated
½ c. walnuts

Preheat oven to 275°. On low mixer speed, combine flour, sugar, margarine and vanilla extract. Then add egg yolk and mix well. Press dough into greased 9" x 13" pan. Brush egg white over dough and sprinkle with walnuts. Bake until brown and then cut into bars.

Vanilla and Jelly Cookies

1½ sticks margarine
1 c. confection sugar
1 egg
½ tsp. vanilla extract
2 c. flour
strawberry jelly

Preheat oven to 350°. Cream margarine with sugar and then add egg and vanilla extract. Mix in flour until soft dough forms. Roll into small balls and place on greased cookie sheet. Make indentation in middle of cookies and fill with jelly. Bake at 350° for 10-15 minutes. Let cool.

Vanilla Cookies

1 c. sugar
2 sticks margarine
2 eggs
2 tsp. lemon juice
2 tsp. vanilla sugar
1 tsp. baking powder
2½ c. flour

Mix all ingredients together. Shape into round balls and place on greased cookie sheet. Bake at 350° for 15 minutes.

White Chocolate Chunk Cookies

1¼ c. flour
¼ tsp. baking soda
⅛ tsp. salt
1 stick margarine
¼ c. sugar
¼ c. brown sugar
1 tsp. vanilla sugar
1 egg
1 c. chopped white chocolate
½ c. chopped walnuts

Combine flour, baking soda and salt. In another bowl, cream margarine with sugar and brown sugar until smooth. Add vanilla sugar and egg. Combine with flour mixture, and then add white chocolate and walnuts. Shape into balls and place on greased cookie sheet. Bake at 375° for 8-10 minutes until golden brown.

Dairy Desserts

Banana Nut Muffins

2 c. flour
¼ c. sugar
1 T. baking powder
½ tsp. salt
1 c. milk
1 egg
½ c. mashed bananas
½ c. chopped walnuts

Preheat oven to 400°. Mix flour, sugar, baking powder and salt in medium bowl. Make a well in the center. In another bowl, mix rest of ingredients, and then pour into center of flour mixture. Combine together, but do not over mix. Pour into greased muffin tins and bake for 20 minutes.

Black & White Balls

1 pkg. sandwich cookies
8 oz. container cream cheese, softened
1 bar dark chocolate
1 bar white chocolate

Combine cookies and cream cheese in blender. Roll into balls and chill for 1 hour in refrigerator. Melt dark chocolate and white chocolate separately, drizzle over balls and refrigerate.

Butter Cookies

1 c. butter
¾ c. sugar
1 egg
1½ tsp. vanilla
2½ c. flour

Mix butter and sugar until creamy, and then add rest of ingredients. Chill for 1 hour in refrigerator. Shape into balls, place on cookie sheet and flatten slightly. Bake at 350° until golden brown.

Cheese Babka

Dough:

2 oz. yeast
1 c. warm water
1 c. sugar
10 c. flour
3 sticks butter
4 egg yolks
2 eggs
1½ c. warm milk

In mixer bowl, dissolve yeast in warm water together with sugar. Let stand for 5 minutes. Add remaining ingredients and mix well. Knead for 5 minutes. Cover and let rise for 1 hour.

Filling:

24 oz. cream cheese, softened
2 lbs. farmer cheese
6 T. vanilla sugar
1 egg
1 egg yolk
1 ½ c. sugar

Combine filling ingredients and mix until smooth. Divide dough into 4 equal portions. Roll out each part into a large rectangle. Spread filling and roll up "jelly roll" style, beginning with wider end. Place in large greased loaf pan.

Crumb Topping:

1 stick butter
1 c. flour
1 c. sugar
1 egg

Combine first 3 topping ingredients by hand to form crumbs. Brush top of babka with egg and sprinkle crumbs on top. Bake at 350° for 45 minutes.

Caramel Cheesecake

16 oz. whipped cream cheese
¾ c. sugar
1 tsp. vanilla sugar
3 eggs
1 graham cracker piecrust

Preheat oven to 350°. Combine all ingredients and pour into crust. Bake for 55 minutes and let cool.

Topping:
1½ bars chocolate
½ tsp. coffee granules
3 T. hot water
1 tsp. light corn syrup

Mix topping ingredients on low flame until consistency is smooth. Pour over cheesecake and refrigerate.

Cheesecake 1

16 oz. whipped cream cheese
4 eggs
1 c. sugar
1 tsp. vanilla sugar
¼ c. flour
1 frozen piecrust

Preheat oven to 375°. Mix all ingredients and pour into piecrust. Turn down oven to 350° and bake for 30 minutes. Then turn off oven and leave in oven until cool.

Topping:
1½ bars white chocolate
½ tsp. coffee dissolved in 3 T. hot water

Melt chocolate together with coffee and pour over cooled cake.

Cheesecake 2

2/3 c. sugar
1/3 c. flour
1 T. cornstarch
1 tsp. vanilla extract
8 oz. whipped cream cheese
2 eggs

Combine sugar, flour and cornstarch. Add in rest of ingredients and mix well. Pour into 9" round tin and bake at 350° until golden brown.

Cheese Danishes

16 oz. whipped cream cheese
1 egg
1/2 c. confection sugar
1 c. sugar
1/2 tsp. vanilla extract
3 oz. white chocolate, melted
1 pkg. flaky dough, precut squares
confection sugar for garnish

Mix together first six ingredients and place a tablespoonful of mixture onto each flaky dough square. Fold both sides together. Place on lined cookie sheet and bake at 350° for 45 minutes. Sprinkle with confection sugar before serving.

Cheese Doughnuts

1 lb. farmer cheese
4 eggs
1/2 c. sugar
1 tsp. baking powder
3/4 c. flour

Combine all ingredients and knead until smooth. Let sit for 10 minutes. Form into balls and deep fry in oil until golden brown. When cool, sprinkle with confection sugar.

Chocolate Cheesecake

Crust:

1 pkg. chocolate sandwich cookies, crushed
6 T. butter, melted

Preheat oven to 325°. Mix crust ingredients together and press into 10" springform pan. Refrigerate.

Filling:

8 oz. softened cream cheese, non-whipped
⅔ c. sugar
3 eggs
12 oz. chocolate chips
8 oz. whip topping
2 T. butter, melted
1 tsp. vanilla

Beat cream cheese and sugar and then add eggs. Mix in rest of filling ingredients and place in crust. Bake at 350° for 1 hour. Allow to cool and then refrigerate.

Chocolate Chip Bars

1¾ c. flour
¾ c. butter, softened
½ c. brown sugar
1 egg
1 tsp. vanilla
2 c. chocolate chips
½ c. chopped pecans

Preheat oven to 350°. Combine all ingredients except chocolate chips and pecans, and then mix in 1 cup chocolate chips by hand. Bake on ungreased pan for 20-30 minutes. Remove from oven and sprinkle remaining chocolate chips on top. Let them melt and spread smoothly over bars. Sprinkle with pecans. Cool and cut into bars.

Dairy Carrot Cake

4 eggs, beaten
2 c. sugar
1 c. applesauce
1½ c. oil
1 tsp. vanilla extract
3 medium carrots, shredded
1 c. chopped walnuts
1 T. ground cinnamon
3 c. flour
1 T. baking soda
1 tsp. salt

Topping:
16 oz. whipped cream cheese
1 c. confection sugar
2 T. vanilla sugar

Mix all cake ingredients and pour into greased bundt pan. Combine topping ingredients and spread on top of batter. Bake uncovered at 350° for 1 hour and 20 minutes.

Dairy Chocolate Cake

2 c. sifted flour
1¾ c. sugar
¾ c. cocoa
1¼ tsp. baking soda
½ tsp. baking powder
¾ c. shortening
¾ c. milk
1 tsp. vanilla sugar
½ c. water
3 eggs

Mix all ingredients and pour into 9" x 13" pan. Bake at 350° for 1 hour.

Dairy Chocolate Chip Muffins

2 c. flour
2 T. sugar
1 T. baking powder
½ tsp. salt
1 egg
1 c. coffee whitener
¼ c. oil
1 c. chocolate chips

Preheat oven to 400°. Mix flour, sugar, baking powder and salt by hand. In separate bowl, beat egg, milk and oil. Combine egg mixture with flour mixture. Do not over mix. Fold in chocolate chips. Pour into greased muffin tins and bake for 20-25 minutes.

Dairy Coffee Cake

2 sticks butter
2 c. sugar
2 eggs
1 c. sour cream
½ tsp. vanilla sugar
2 c. flour
1 tsp. baking powder
¼ tsp. salt

Cream butter and sugar and then add eggs. Mix in remaining ingredients and pour ⅓ cup of batter into greased bundt pan.

Filling:
1 c. chopped pecans
3 T. sugar
1 tsp. cinnamon

Combine filling ingredients and sprinkle ¾ of mixture on top of batter. Pour in rest of batter and top with remaining nut mixture. Bake at 350° for 1 hour.

Doughnuts

2 eggs
2 T. sugar
½ tsp. salt
1 c. vanilla yogurt
1 T. baking powder
2 c. flour
confection sugar

Mix eggs, sugar and salt on medium speed. Add yogurt, baking powder and flour. Mix until batter forms. Drop batter in hot oil (enough to cover doughnuts) and fry until golden brown. Allow doughnuts to cool and sprinkle with confection sugar.

Easy Chocolate Mousse

1½ c. miniature marshmallows
⅓ c. milk
1 c. chocolate chips
¾ c. whip topping
⅛ tsp. almond extract

Heat marshmallows and milk in small pot over low flame and mix well until all marshmallows have melted. Melt in chocolate chips, and then remove from heat and let cool. Beat whip topping until stiff and set half aside. Fold chocolate mixture into other half of whipped topping and spoon into 4 glasses. Fold almond extract into remaining whipped topping and spoon onto mixture. Chill before serving.

Jelly Muffins

2 c. flour, sifted
1 T. baking powder
1/8 tsp. salt
1/2 c. sugar
2 eggs
1 c. milk
4 T. butter, melted
1 tsp. vanilla extract
Strawberry jelly

Preheat oven to 400°. Combine flour, baking powder and salt and then mix in sugar. In another bowl, beat eggs, milk, butter and vanilla extract. Make a hole in dry ingredients and pour liquid mixture into hole. Stir gently. Spoon half of batter into cupcake holders in muffin tin. Top with jelly and spoon remaining batter over jelly. Bake for 45 minutes or until golden brown.

Lowfat Cheesecake

1 lb. farmer cheese
8 oz. sour cream
3 eggs
1 c. sugar
3 T. flour
1 tsp. vanilla sugar
1 graham cracker piecrust

Mix all ingredients and place into crust. Bake at 350° for 30 minutes.

Strawberry Muffins

2¼ c. flour
⅓ c. sugar
3 tsp. baking powder
½ tsp. salt
2 eggs
½ c. oil
½ c. milk
1 tsp. vanilla sugar
1 c. diced strawberries

Combine flour, sugar, baking powder and salt. In another bowl, beat eggs, oil, milk and vanilla sugar. Add to dry ingredients and then fold in strawberries. Pour into greased cupcake holders and bake at 400° for 25 minutes or until slightly golden on top.

Super Cookies

1 c. butter, softened
¾ c. sugar
¾ c. light brown sugar
1 tsp. vanilla sugar
2 eggs
2½ c. flour
1 tsp. baking soda
½ tsp. salt
1 c. chocolate chips
½ c. coconut flakes
½ c. oatmeal
½ c. raisins

Cream butter and all sugars until fluffy, and then add eggs. In another bowl, combine flour, baking soda and salt. Add to liquid ingredients and beat well. Mix in rest of ingredients. Shape into small balls and place onto ungreased cookie sheet. Flatten cookies and bake at 375° for 8-10 minutes.

Toffee Bars

2 c. sugar
2 sticks butter, softened
¼ c. water
½ tsp. salt
1 T. vanilla extract
2 c. chocolate chips
1 c. chopped pecans

Place sugar, butter, water and salt into a pot and bring to a boil (should be caramel color). Remove from heat and mix in vanilla extract until bubbling stops. Spread mixture onto cookie sheet that has been lined with parchment paper and sprayed with Pam. Allow to cool. Melt chocolate chips and spread over toffee. Sprinkle pecans on top and cut into bars when cool.

Triangle Cheesecake

¾ lb. farmer cheese
½ stick margarine, softened
½ c. sugar
2 eggs
¼ c. milk
¼ c. sweet wine
15 light tea biscuits
15 dark tea biscuits

Mix farmer cheese, margarine, sugar and eggs and set aside. Combine milk and wine and dip biscuits into mixture. Layer biscuits on aluminum foil, 3 columns of 4 biscuits each. Put cheese mixture on top, then another layer of biscuits and another layer of cheese. With your hands under the foil, gently bring outer columns up and together to form a long pyramid. Freeze.

Ice Cream and Ices

Chocolate Swirl Milkshake (dairy)

3 c. vanilla ice cream
3 c. milk
3/4 tsp. vanilla extract
3/4 c. chocolate syrup

Combine ice cream, milk and vanilla extract in blender until thick. Pour chocolate syrup on bottom of glasses and drizzle in spiral pattern around inside of glasses. Apportion milk shake equally into each glass.

Coconut Rice Krispies® Ice Cream Squares (dairy or pareve)

1 stick margarine
3/4 c. shredded coconut
2 1/2 c. Rice Krispies®
3/4 c. brown sugar
1/2 gal. vanilla ice cream (dairy or pareve)

Melt margarine in a 9" x 13" pan and set aside. In a bowl, combine coconut, Rice Krispies and brown sugar and spread onto cookie sheet. Bake at 350° for 25-30 minutes. Cool. Make a vanilla ice cream of your choice or use store-bought ice cream. Place half of Rice Krispies mixture on bottom of pan with melted margarine. Cover with ice cream and then with remaining mixture. Freeze. Cut into squares and serve.

Coffee Ice Cream (pareve)

16 oz. whip topping, whipped
½ c. confection sugar
3 eggs
2 heaping T. vanilla sugar
2 ½ T. coffee, dissolved in water
1 capful Godiva® chocolate

Mix whipped topping, confection sugar, eggs and vanilla sugar. Combine coffee with chocolate and add to mixture. Freeze.

Cookies & Cream Ice Cream 1 (pareve)

4 eggs, separated
16 oz. whip topping
½ c. sugar
2 T. vanilla sugar, or as desired
8-10 sandwich cookies, crushed

Whip egg whites and set aside. In another bowl, beat whip topping and add sugar, vanilla sugar and egg yolks. Fold egg whites into whipped mixture. Mix in cookies and freeze.

Cookies & Cream Ice Cream 2 (pareve)

16 oz. whip topping, whipped
½ c. sugar
4 eggs
2 tsp. vanilla extract
20 black and white sandwich cookies, crushed

Mix first four ingredients. Freeze 45 minutes to 1 hour. Mix crushed sandwich cookies into ice cream and refreeze.

Cookies & Cream Ice Cream Pie (pareve)

16 oz. whip topping, whipped
¼ c. sugar
2 eggs
1 tsp. vanilla sugar
10 sandwich cookies, crushed
1 chocolate piecrust

Mix whip topping, sugar, eggs and vanilla sugar and freeze for 45 minutes. Combine with cookies. Pour into chocolate piecrust and refreeze.

Cookie Dough Ice Cream (pareve)

16 oz. whip topping
2 eggs
½ pkg. chocolate pudding mix
1 tsp. vanilla sugar
1 pkg. soft bake chocolate chip cookies, crushed

Beat whip, eggs, pudding mix and vanilla sugar until stiff. Fold in crushed cookies. Pour into 9" x 13" pan and freeze.

Creamsicle Milkshake (dairy)

4 c. vanilla ice cream
2 c. orange juice
4 T. sugar
4 T. milk
2 tsp. vanilla extract

Blend all ingredients in blender and serve in glasses.

Creamsicle Roll (pareve)

Ices:
1 large coffee whitener
1 jello mix (cherry or orange)

Ice Cream:
6 eggs, separated
3/4 c. sugar
16 oz. whip topping
2 T. vanilla sugar

Combine whitener and jello mix until dissolved. Pour onto lined cookie sheet and freeze. Beat egg whites until stiff. Add sugar and set aside. Beat whip topping and then add yolks and vanilla sugar. Fold egg whites into whip mixture and then freeze for a few hours or overnight. Take jello mixture and whip mixture out of freezer and allow to soften slightly. Spread whip mixture on top of jello mixture. Either roll up "jelly roll" style or leave as is. Refreeze and cut into squares.

Crunchy Ice Cream (dairy or pareve)

3½ oz. bar white chocolate (dairy or pareve)
½ c. peanut butter
1½ c. corn flakes
1 gal. vanilla ice cream (dairy or pareve)

Melt chocolate with peanut butter and crumble in corn flakes. Mix into slightly melted ice cream and refreeze.

Frozen Chocolate or Vanilla Pops (dairy)

⅓ c. sugar
2½ c. milk
1 pkg. chocolate or vanilla instant pudding mix

Beat all ingredients until thick. Pour into ice pop holders and freeze.

Fudgesicles (dairy)

1 c. milk
5 eggs
1½ sticks margarine
1 c. sugar
3 T. cocoa

Blend all ingredients in blender. Pour into cups and freeze. When halfway frozen, insert a stick into each cup and refreeze.

Ice Cream Crunch Mix (pareve)

Crunch:

1 stick margarine, softened
½ c. brown sugar
½ tsp. coffee granules
½ tsp. vanilla
1¼ c. flour
¼ tsp. baking powder
½ c. chocolate chips

Mix all ingredients in blender. Spread onto lined cookie sheet and bake at 350° for 20 minutes. When cool, break into small pieces.

Ice Cream:

5 eggs, separated
¾ c. sugar
16 oz. whip topping
1 tsp. vanilla extract

Beat egg whites until stiff. In another bowl, beat egg yolks with sugar. In a third bowl, whip up whip. Mix everything together. Fold in crunch pieces and freeze.

Ice Cream Pie (pareve)

4 eggs
¼ c. sugar
1 bar Rosemarie® chocolate
1 stick margarine
1 graham cracker piecrust
8 oz. whip topping

Beat eggs and sugar and set aside. Melt chocolate and margarine over low flame. Combine all ingredients, pour into crust and freeze. Whip up topping, spread over pie and refreeze.

Ice Cream Sandwich (dairy or pareve)

1 pkg. chocolate chip cookies
Ice cream (any flavor, dairy or pareve)
Topping (sprinkles, chopped nuts, shredded coconut, chocolate chips, etc.)

Place ice cream in between two cookies and roll edges in any topping desired. Freeze.

Mango Sorbet (pareve)

2 mangos, peeled and cubed
3 T. sugar
2 tsp. lemon juice

Beat mangos, sugar and lemon juice. Freeze partially. Re-beat and refreeze.

Napoleon (pareve)

2 c. coffee whitener
2 pkgs. vanilla instant pudding mix
16 oz. whip topping
1 box graham crackers

Mix coffee whitener and pudding mix. Whip up whip topping and fold into pudding mixture. In greased 9" x 13" pan, layer crackers, whip mixture, crackers, whip mixture and crackers. Freeze.

Topping:
6 T. cocoa
2 T. corn syrup
3 T. margarine, softened
2 T. vanilla sugar
2 T. oil
1½ c. confection sugar
3 T. coffee whitener

Mix topping ingredients. After the Napoleon is frozen, pour on top.

Pareve Coffee Ice Cream
(pareve)

6 eggs, separated
¾ c. sugar
16 oz. whip topping
1 tsp. vanilla sugar
3 T. coffee granules
6 T. hot water

Beat egg whites with sugar until stiff. At slow speed, add egg yolks, one at a time. Beat whip topping and fold into mixture. Dissolve coffee in water, then blend coffee into mixture and freeze.

Raspberry Ice Cream
(pareve)

32 oz. whip topping
2 boxes Birdseye frozen raspberries
1 large jar marshmallow fluff

Beat all ingredients together and freeze.

Rice Krispies® Ice Cream Squares (pareve)

Ice cream:

16 oz. whip topping
1 egg yolk
½ c. sugar
1 tsp. coffee
¼ c. hot water

Whip up whip topping, and then add egg yolk and sugar. In another bowl, beat egg whites until stiff. Fold egg whites into whip mixture. Dissolve coffee in water, fold in coffee and mix well.

Rice Krispies:

1 stick margarine
4 T. brown sugar
3 c. Rice Krispies®

Melt margarine in pan with brown sugar. Mix in Rice Krispies and put in greased 9" x 13" pan. Put into oven for 5 minutes at 350°. Remove from oven, allow to cool, and then crumble the mixture and divide into two portions. Place half the crumbled mixture back into the pan, cover with ice cream and place the remaining crumble on top. Refreeze. Serve in squares.

Sorbet (pareve)

1 c. water
1 pkg. jello mix (any flavor)
1 c. orange juice
1 c. pineapple juice

Bring water to boil and dissolve jello mix in water. Then mix in orange juice and pineapple juice. Pour into 9" x 13" pan and freeze. When frozen, remove from freezer and allow to thaw enough that it can be beaten again. Beat until fluffy and then refreeze.

To make sorbet rainbow squares, repeat above directions using three different jello colors. Lay one on top of another and then cut into squares.

Strawberry Ice Cream (pareve)

1 container frozen strawberries, defrosted
16 oz. whip topping, whipped
1 large jar marshmallow fluff

Blend all ingredients and freeze in container.

Strawberry Sorbet (pareve)

1 bag frozen strawberries without syrup, defrosted
½ c. sugar
1 c. orange juice

Blend all ingredients and freeze in container. When frozen halfway, blend again and refreeze.

Three-Layer Ices (pareve)

3 pkgs. jello mix (red, orange and yellow)
16 oz. whip topping

For each color jello:
½ c. sugar
1 c. orange juice
1 c. pineapple juice
1 c. boiling water

Prepare each colored jello separately by combining jello mix with other ingredients except whip topping. Freeze each color in a separate bowl. Take out first color and beat until fluffy. Pour into bottom of 9" x 13" pan and refreeze. When frozen, put layer of whip topping on top. Take out second color and repeat. Take out last color and repeat, but do not put on whip topping. Freeze until serving.

Vanilla Ice Cream (pareve)

20 oz. whip topping
6 eggs
1 c. sugar
3 tsp. vanilla

Beat until thick and freeze in container.

Vanilla Milkshakes (dairy)

2 c. milk
3 scoops vanilla ice cream
1 ice cube
4 oz. whipped cream

Blend milk, ice cream and ice cube in blender until smooth. Top with whipped cream.

Vanilla Strawberry Ice Cream (pareve)

1 c. coffee whitener
1 8 oz. whip topping, *not* whipped
1 pkg. vanilla instant pudding mix
16 oz. frozen strawberries in syrup
1½ c. orange juice
1½ c. sugar

Blend coffee whitener with whip and instant pudding mix. Mix well and freeze for 3 hours. Beat 8 oz. strawberries with 1 c. sugar and 1 c. orange juice. Pour over frozen vanilla pudding. Blend remaining orange juice, sugar and strawberries and refrigerate. Pour on ice cream right before serving.

Viennese Ice Cream (pareve)

16 oz. whip topping
1 egg
½ small jar marshmallow fluff
10 Viennese crunch, chopped
1 chocolate graham cracker piecrust

Whip up whip topping. Add remaining ingredients and mix well. Pour into crust and freeze.

Mousses and Pies

Blueberry Pie

2 c. flour
2 tsp. baking powder
¾ c. sugar
1 stick margarine
1 egg
1 tsp. vanilla sugar
1 can blueberry pie filling

Mix all ingredients except blueberry filling and form into crumbs. Place crumbs on bottom of 9" round pan, leaving some for topping. Pour pie filling on top and sprinkle with remaining crumbs. Bake at 350° for 1 hour.

Boston Cream Pie

3 squares chocolate
1 stick margarine
2 eggs
1 c. confection sugar
1 graham cracker piecrust

Partially melt chocolate together with margarine in microwave. Then add rest of ingredients and mix well. Pour into graham cracker piecrust and freeze.

Topping:
16 oz. whip topping, whipped
1 tsp. vanilla sugar
3 T. confection sugar

Mix topping ingredients and spread on top of pie.

Chocolate Chip Pie 1

Crust:

1 pkg. Ostreicher's® chocolate chip cookies
1 stick margarine

Blend ingredients and spread into 9" round pan. Bake at 350° for 10 minutes and let cool.

Filling:

1½ sticks margarine
6 oz. chocolate chips, melted
6 eggs
3 c. confection sugar
3 tsp. vanilla extract

Melt together margarine and chocolate chips and then beat in rest of ingredients. Pour into piecrust and freeze for 1 hour.

Topping:

8 oz. whip topping
2 eggs, separated
1½ T. vanilla sugar
1 tsp. coffee granules
small amount of water
2 T. sugar
handful cookies, crushed

Beat whip topping with egg yolks and vanilla sugar. Dissolve coffee in water and add to whip mixture. Beat egg whites with sugar until stiff and combine with whip mixture. Pour over frozen pie and sprinkle with crushed cookies.

Chocolate Chip Pie 2

2 eggs
½ c. flour
½ c. sugar
½ c. brown sugar
¾ stick margarine
¼ c. chocolate chips
ice cream, if desired
1 graham cracker piecrust

Mix all ingredients well and pour into piecrust. Bake at 350° for 35 to 40 minutes. Can also be made in individual graham cracker crusts. Serve warm with any flavor ice cream.

Chocolate Eclairs

Puffs:
1 stick margarine
1 c. water, boiled
1 c. flour
4 eggs

Combine margarine with boiled water in pot over low flame, stirring until melted. Add flour and mix briskly until smooth. Remove from heat and let cool. Pour into mixer and then add eggs one at a time, mixing well. Drop spoonfuls onto greased baking sheet and bake at 350° for 35 minutes or until golden brown.

Cream:
5 egg yolks
2 sticks margarine
10 tsp. confection sugar
1 T. rum
3 T. cocoa
1 bar bittersweet chocolate

Mix first five ingredients well. When puffs have cooled, slit them halfway and fill with cream. Melt chocolate and drizzle on top. Refrigerate.

Chocolate Cream Pie

Piecrust:
1½ c. flour
1 egg
1 tsp. vanilla sugar
¼ c. sugar
⅛ tsp. salt
⅓ c. oil
1 tsp. baking powder
1 T. cocoa

Mix piecrust ingredients into a dough and press into lined 9" round tin. Prick holes in dough with fork. Bake at 350° for 25 minutes.

Filling:
12 oz. chocolate chips
1 T. wine
4 eggs
1 T. flour
¼ c. water
1 pkg. vanilla instant pudding mix

Melt chocolate chips in pot. Blend rest of ingredients, add melted chocolate and then mix well. Spread filling into crust and freeze.

Topping:
8 oz. whip topping
1 T. confection sugar
chocolate curls

Whip up whip topping and then add confection sugar. Spread onto pie and garnish with chocolate curls.

Chocolate Mint Pie

6 eggs, separated
8 oz. whip topping
1 c. confection sugar
1 tsp. vanilla sugar
2 tsp. peppermint extract
green food coloring
1 c. grated chocolate
2 piecrusts

Whip egg whites until stiff. In another bowl, slowly beat egg yolks and whip topping. Add confection sugar, vanilla sugar, peppermint extract and food coloring, mixing well. Fold in egg whites, and then mix in chocolate by hand. Spread into piecrusts and freeze.

Chocolate Mousse Pie

7 oz. chocolate (good quality bars)
16 oz. marshmallows
½ c. coffee whitener
16 oz. whip topping
1 graham cracker piecrust

Place chocolate, marshmallows and milk in pot and melt over low flame. Allow to cool. Whip up whip topping and fold into chocolate mixture. Pour into piecrust and freeze. Allow to defrost slightly before serving.

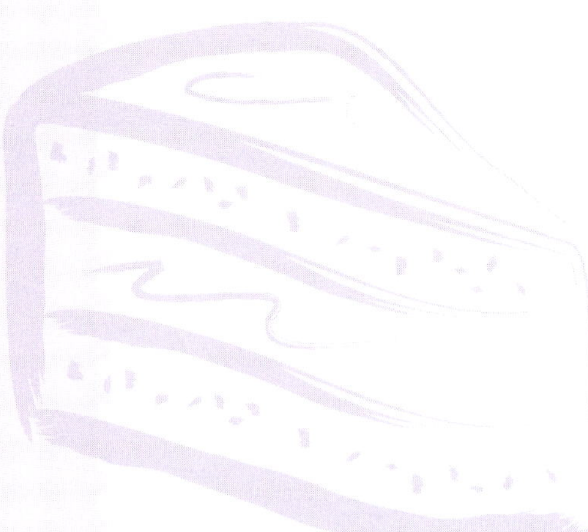

Chocolate Pie

1 piecrust
1 c. chocolate chips
¼ c. water
1½ c. sugar
2 eggs
16 oz. whip topping

Bake piecrust according to directions. Melt chocolate chips with water in microwave or over double boiler. Mix in sugar and eggs. Whip up whip topping and fold half into mixture. Place mixture in piecrust and freeze. When frozen, spread remaining whip topping over pie.

Cookies & Cream Pie 1

32 oz. whip topping
2 egg whites
½ c. sugar
2 tsp. vanilla sugar
10 sandwich cookies, crushed
2 chocolate graham cracker piecrusts

Whip up whip. Beat in egg whites, sugar and vanilla sugar. When mixed well, add crushed cookies. Pour into piecrusts and freeze.

Cookies & Cream Pie 2

16 oz. whip topping
½ c. sugar
4 eggs
2 tsp. vanilla sugar
20 chocolate sandwich cookies, crushed
3 chocolate graham cracker piecrusts

Whip up whip topping. Add sugar, eggs and vanilla sugar and then fold in crushed cookies. Pour into piecrusts and freeze.

Easy Peanut Butter Pie

1 chocolate graham cracker piecrust
2-3 c. vanilla ice cream
2-3 c. chocolate ice cream
1 c. peanut butter (chilled)
chocolate sauce or syrup

Chill piecrust. Mix both ice creams together. Quickly mix in peanut butter. Place mixture in piecrust. Drizzle chocolate sauce or chocolate syrup over ice cream. Freeze well.

Lemon Pie

16 oz. whip topping
1 lemon pie filling
1 large jar marshmallow fluff
1 graham cracker piecrust

Whip up whip topping, and then add lemon pie filling and marshmallow fluff. Pour into piecrust and freeze.

Lemon Tarts

1 piecrust
1½ c. whip topping
1 jar lemon pie filling
2 tsp. sugar
fresh strawberries or raspberries

Bake piecrust as directed. Whip up whip topping, and then mix in lemon pie filling and sugar. When piecrust has cooled, pour mixture into piecrust. Garnish with fresh strawberries or raspberries. (Can also be made as individual pies.)

Mud Pies

16 oz. whip topping
2 eggs, separated
1 c. sugar
1 tsp. vanilla sugar
1½ tsp. coffee, dissolved in hot water
2 graham cracker piecrusts

Whip up whip topping and set aside. Beat egg whites until stiff and then add rest of ingredients. Fold in whip by hand. Pour into piecrusts and freeze.

Topping:
⅓ c. cocoa
⅔ c. sugar
4 oz. whip topping
2 T. margarine

Put topping ingredients in pot and mix over low flame until it thickens. Pour over frozen pie.

Peanut Butter Chocolate Pie

16 oz. whip topping
1 box chocolate instant pudding mix
1 graham cracker piecrust

Whip up whip topping until stiff. Add in pudding mix and mix well. Pour into piecrust.

Topping:
⅓ c. light corn syrup
½ c. chunky peanut butter
⅓ c. chocolate syrup

Mix topping ingredients and spread on top of pie. Freeze.

Peanut Butter Ice Cream Pie

1/3 c. peanut butter
2 c. Rice Krispies®
1 gal. vanilla ice cream

Stir ingredients until well blended. Spread mixture into 9" pie pan and chill. Fill with vanilla ice cream and freeze.

Peanut Butter Mousse

Crust:

1 pkg. tea biscuits, crushed
1/2 c. margarine
3 T. brown sugar

Mix above ingredients, place in 9" x 13" pan and bake at 350° for 5-10 minutes. Allow to cool.

Ice Cream:

5 eggs, separated
3/4 c. sugar
12 oz. whip topping

Whip egg whites and sugar until stiff. Beat together yolks and whip topping. Combine both mixtures. Pour onto crust and freeze.

Topping:

1/2 c. chocolate syrup
1/2 c. crunchy peanut butter
1/2 c. light corn syrup

Mix topping ingredients and pour over pie. Refreeze.

Pecan Pie 1

3 eggs, beaten
1 c. corn syrup
1 c. sugar
1 T. margarine, melted
1 tsp. vanilla
1½ c. pecans
1 piecrust

Combine first five ingredients until well blended. Stir in pecans. Pour into piecrust and bake at 350° for 50-55 minutes.

Pecan Pie 2

3 eggs, slightly beaten
1 c. sugar
1 c. light corn syrup
2 T. margarine, melted
1 tsp. vanilla sugar
2 piecrusts
2 c. chopped pecans
ice cream

Mix first five ingredients and divide batter into both piecrusts. Put pecans on top. Bake at 350° for 50 minutes to 1 hour. (Serve warm with ice cream.)

Pecan Pie 3

1 tsp. vanilla sugar
2 T. margarine, melted
1 c. light corn syrup
1 c. sugar
3 eggs, slightly beaten
2 piecrusts
2 c. chopped pecans

Mix all ingredients. Pour into piecrusts. Sprinkle pecans on top. Bake at 350° for 50 minutes to 1 hour.

Rosemarie Mousse Pie

2 eggs
3½ bar Rosemarie® chocolate
¾ stick margarine
¾ c. confection sugar
1 graham cracker piecrust

Beat eggs and set aside. Melt chocolate and margarine, pour in bowl and then add sugar and eggs. Mix well. Pour into piecrust. Freeze.

Topping:
8 oz. whip topping
3 T. confection sugar

Whip up whip topping with confection sugar. When pie is frozen, pour topping over and refreeze.

Simple Chocolate or Vanilla Pie

chocolate or vanilla instant pudding mix
1 graham cracker piecrust
8 oz. whip topping, whipped
Topping (sprinkles, chopped nuts, shredded coconut, chocolate chips, etc.)

Prepare pudding according to package directions and pour into crust. Garnish with whip topping and sprinkle with topping of your choice.

Strawberry Mousse

1 bag frozen strawberries, defrosted
1 c. sugar
2 eggs
1 tsp. vanilla sugar
1 tsp. orange juice
16 oz. whip topping
2 graham cracker piecrusts

Beat all ingredients together. Add whip topping and whip until thick. Pour into graham cracker piecrusts. Freeze.

Three-Layer Mousse

6 eggs, separated
1 c. sugar
1 stick margarine
7 oz. chocolate chips
1 vanilla sugar
8 oz. whip topping
4 T. confection sugar

Mix ¾ c. sugar with egg yolks. Melt together margarine, chocolate chips and vanilla sugar. Pour mixture into yolks. In another bowl, beat egg whites until stiff. Add remaining sugar. Combine chocolate mixture with egg whites. Pour half in round pan. Bake at 350° for 30 minutes. Refrigerate remaining batter. When cake cools, place mousse on top and freeze. Whip up whip topping with confection sugar and spread on mousse. Refreeze.

Tollhouse Cookie Pie

2 eggs
½ c. flour
½ c. sugar
½ c. brown sugar
1½ sticks margarine
1 c. chocolate chips
1 piecrust

Beat eggs and then add rest of ingredients. Pour into piecrust. Bake at 325° for 55 minutes.

Two-Tone Pudding Pie

1 vanilla pudding mix
1 chocolate pudding mix
1 chocolate graham cracker piecrust
rice dream or soy milk
8 oz. whip topping
Chocolate sprinkles/curls

Make one box of pudding according to package directions. Pour into crust and let cool. Make other pudding and pour over first. When cooled, whip up whip topping and pour over pudding. Sprinkle with chocolate sprinkles or chocolate curls.

Viennese Mousse Pie

12 eggs, separated
1½ c. sugar
10½ oz. Noblesse® chocolate bars
3 sticks margarine
20 oz. whip topping
8-10 Viennese crunch, chopped

Preheat oven to 350°. Beat egg whites with ¾ c. sugar until stiff. Set aside. In another bowl, beat egg yolks with rest of sugar. Mix chocolate and margarine on low flame and then add into egg mixture. Fold in egg whites and mix slowly. Place half of mixture into two 9" round pans. Put remaining batter in refrigerator. Bake at 350° for 25 minutes and then let cool. Remove batter from refrigerator, spread over cake and freeze. Beat whip topping, spread on pie, sprinkle Viennese crunch on top and refreeze.

Drinks and Fruit Desserts

Ambrosia

8 oz. whip topping, *not* whipped
1 box frozen strawberries, defrosted
20 oz. can crushed pineapple, undrained

Combine together whip topping and strawberries and then mix in pineapple. Chill in refrigerator.

Apple Compote

8 Cortland apples, peeled and sliced
4 large plums, unpeeled, cut into chunks
⅔ c. water
sugar to taste

Put apples, plums and water in pot and bring to a boil. Lower heat and simmer for 1 hour. Add sugar to taste and mix well.

Banana Milkshake

1 banana
1 tsp. sugar
1 c. milk
1 scoop vanilla ice cream

Puree banana and sugar in blender. Add milk and ice cream and blend. Pour into glass. If desired, add a scoop of ice cream on top.

Candy Apples

6 apples
½ c. light corn syrup
2 c. sugar
¾ c. water
red food coloring

Put sugar, corn syrup and water into pot. Mix over low flame until sugar dissolves. Add drops of red food coloring. Let set for 15 minutes. Insert skewer into bottom part of each apple. Dip apples into mixture and place on waxed paper until they become hard and dry.

Optional: Sprinkle with shredded coconut or nuts.

Coffee Drink

½ gal. milk
sugar (as desired)
8 oz. whip topping
3 T. coffee granules dissolved in 6 T. hot water

Blend all ingredients and chill.

Easy Strawberry Crepes

1 pkg. ready-made crepes
fresh strawberries, sliced
¼ c. confection sugar
8 oz. whip topping

Prepare crepes according to directions. Puree strawberries with sugar and chill. Whip up whip topping and spread on crepes. Fold crepes in half and drizzle strawberry sauce over crepes or on plates.

Fruit Cup

2 oranges, sliced
2 kiwis, cubed
½ small box strawberries
1 c. red grapes

Sauce:
½ c. orange juice
½ c. sugar
⅓ c. lemon juice

Arrange fruits in bowl. Place sauce ingredients in pot and bring to a boil. Let cool. Pour over fruit and marinate in refrigerator before serving.

Fruit Mix

15 oz. crushed pineapple
15 oz. apple sauce
1 bag frozen strawberries (with syrup), defrosted
1 strawberry jello mix, combined with a drop of hot water

Blend first three ingredients and then mix in jello. Chill.

Fruit Trifle

Fruits as desired
1 bag frozen strawberries (with syrup), defrosted

Layer any fruits desired in a glass trifle bowl. Puree frozen strawberries and set aside.

Crunch:
2 c. Rice Krispies®
1 stick margarine, melted
1 c. sugar
1 c. roasted ground almonds

Mix all ingredients, pour into pan and bake at 350° for 20 minutes. Before serving trifle, pour pureed strawberries (and/or raspberry sauce – see below) over fruit and top with crunch. (Can also be arranged and served on individual plates.)

Raspberry Sauce (optional):
⅔ c. sugar
⅔ c. water
1 T. cornstarch
1 box frozen raspberries, defrosted

Put sugar, water and cornstarch in pot and mix over medium flame until smooth. Add raspberries and bring to a boil. Remove from heat and allow to cool. Refrigerate. Drizzle over fruit trifle.

Iced Coffee

5 c. milk
2 tsp. coffee granules, flavored
1 T. vanilla sugar
10 tsp. sugar
1 c. boiling water
vanilla or coffee ice cream

Blend all ingredients. Pour into tall glasses. Serve with scoop of ice cream.

Iced Malted

1 tsp. coffee granules
1 pkg. chocolate instant pudding mix
¼ c. boiling water
½ gal. cold milk
1½ c. sugar
ice cream

Dissolve coffee and pudding mix into boiling water. Add milk and sugar, blend together and then refrigerate. Serve in a glass with a scoop of ice cream.

Pina Colada Drink

1 container frozen strawberries (with syrup), defrosted
8 oz. whip topping
1 can pineapple juice
1 c. Pina Colada

Blend strawberries and whip topping. Add pineapple juice and Pina Colada and mix well.

Pineapple Slush

1 qt. orange juice
½ c. lemon juice
1 c. white wine
1 c. crushed pineapple
1 c. sugar
Sprite soda

Blend all ingredients. Let stand for 1 hour and then freeze. Blend again and refreeze. Serve in individual cups partially frozen. Pour Sprite over slush before serving.

Strawberry Daiquiri

8 whole fresh strawberries
6 ice cubes
2 oz. pineapple juice
1 oz. fresh lime juice
sugar as desired

Blend all ingredients until smooth.

Strawberry Mango Drink

9 ripe mangos, peeled and diced
1 box Ceres® mango drink
5 bags frozen strawberries (without syrup), defrosted
1 c. sugar

Blend mangos in food processor. Add mango drink and blend again. Blend strawberries with sugar in food processor and pour into pitcher.

Strawberry Peach Smoothie

1 bag frozen strawberries (with syrup), defrosted
1 small can peaches with juice
3 T. orange juice
whip cream

Blend all ingredients. Top with whip cream.

Index of Recipes

Index of Recipes

Index of Recipes

Notes/Personal Recipes

Notes/Personal Recipes

Notes/Personal Recipes

Notes/Personal Recipes

Notes/Personal Recipes

Notes/Personal Recipes